I'm Adopted, You're Adopted

To order additional copies of
I'M ADOPTED, YOU'RE ADOPTED
by
Susan Davis,
call
1-800-765-6955.
Visit us at
www.reviewandherald.com
for information on other Review and Herald®
products.

I'm Adopted, You're Adopted

Susan Davis

Autumn
House® Publishing
www.autumnhousepublishing.com
A Division of **REVIEW AND HERALD® PUBLISHING**
Since 1861

Copyright © 2007 by Review and Herald® Publishing Association

Published by Autumn House® Publishing, a division of Review and Herald®
Publishing, Hagerstown, MD 21741-1119

The author assumes full responsibility for the accuracy of all facts and quotations as
cited in this book.

Bible texts credited to Clear Word/Kids are from *The Clear Word
for Kids,* copyright © 2005 by Review and Herald Publishing Association.
All rights reserved.

This book was
Edited by Penny Estes Wheeler
Designed by Ron Pride
Cover art by Andrei Vieira
Typeset: Bembo 14.5/17.5

PRINTED IN U.S.A.
11 10 09 08 07   5 4 3 2 1

Library of Congress Cataloging-in-Publication Data
Davis, Susan, 1942-   .
  I'm adopted, you're adopted / Susan Davis.
      p. cm.
  Summary: With the impending arrival of his new little sister, Jeffie learns about
adoption and the specialness of being chosen, just like his adoption
into God's family.
  ISBN 978-0-8127-0434-1
  [1. Adoption—Fiction. 2. Christian life—Fiction.] I. Title.   II. Title: I am
adopted, you are adopted.
  PZ7.D317Iam 2007
  [Fic]—dc22
                              2006035117

To

Jim *and* Chuck, *my adopted brothers,*

and Forrest, *my adopted son.*

To adopted children around the world;

and to those who wait in hope to find a family—

this book is dedicated.

Dear Caring Adult,

This is a story about being adopted, about needing a family to call one's own.

About being loved and belonging.

About God's dearest wish for each of His children.

And this is a story about death and sadness. About teaching a child simply and honestly about death so he will ever after have a foundation upon which to rest his faith, a cornerstone of truth upon which to rebuild his life after the loss of a loved one.

This is a story about life and hope and joy and belonging.

"Because He loved us so,

He decided to secure our future

by adopting us as His children.

This happened to His plan through Jesus."

—*Ephesians 1:5,* Clear Word for Kids

Contents

A Sister for Jeffie

Chapter 1

Jeffie picked up his spoon and stirred the cereal around in his bowl. "Mom, when is Sandi coming?" he asked, just as he did almost every morning.

"Only 54 days now, Jeffie," Mom said after she'd checked the calendar. "That is seven and a half weeks."

As Jeffie ate, he thought of what had happened since he had turned 6. The biggest thing was that his little brother Morrie had gotten sick and died. That had been a hard time for Jeffie.

The house seemed empty without his 4-year-old brother. His heart was empty too. He missed playing with Morrie, and he'd cried a lot.

Mom had told him that it was all right to cry. Sometimes she and Daddy cried too. They liked to talk about Morrie, and to remember the fun things they'd done together. Jeffie and his parents talked about Morrie often. They talked, too, of being together in heaven. As the months passed, Jeffie began to feel better. He could think of Morrie without crying because he knew his little brother was only resting. He was waiting for Jesus to come and wake him up.

It was about then that Mom told him about Sandi, the little girl they were planning to adopt. At once, Jeffie had been excited. He helped do many things to get ready for Sandi.

Daddy had painted the room that used to be Morrie's a soft pink. Mom bought pretty curtains for the windows and made a patchwork quilt for the bed. They found pictures a little girl would like, to hang on the wall. The old dresser was painted white, and inside were little undershirts and panties and socks. The bottom drawer held extra blankets and sheets for the bed.

Jeffie was saving his allowance, too. He wanted to buy Sandi a special doll he'd seen at the store. It had brown hair and brown eyes, just like Sandi's. He wanted to have the doll ready for her the day she came.

———◆———

"Meow" came a sound from outside the door. "Meow, meow."

Jeffie slid off his stool and ran to open the door. Frosty, his white cat, ran in. "Meow!" she said, looking right at Jeffie. "Mama, Frosty wants her food right now," Jeffie told her. He picked up a box and poured dry cat food into Frosty's dish and set it on the floor. She ate with small crunching sounds.

"Frosty sure has grown since we got her," he said. He looked back in his mind and remembered a tiny white kitten. "Mama, do you remember when she came to our house?" he asked.

"I surely do," Mom said. "It was the night of the big storm. She was small, but she meowed so loudly that we heard her even above the thunder!"

"I was scared of the thunder," Jeffie said with a little shiver. "But when I heard her, it made me forget the storm. I opened the door—and there sat this cat. Only she was a kitten then."

Mom laughed. "It was hard to tell *what* she was. She was so dirty and wet and ragged-looking."

"*I* knew right away that it was a kitten," said Jeffie. "Even if she did look skinny and wet. She came right to me and meowed some more. She was saying, 'I'm scared! Isn't anybody going to help me? I'm hungry, too.' So I poured milk for her. After she ate and dried out she didn't look so bad."

"She's turned into a pretty cat," Mom agreed.

"Did you hear that?" Jeffie asked as he picked up Frosty and wiped a drop of milk from her whiskers. "You are a pretty cat." Frosty purred as she licked her paws and washed her face with them.

Jeffie had a faraway look in his eyes. He was thinking. "Mama," he said after a while, "taking Frosty in and giving her a home is adopting her, isn't it?"

"Yes," she said. She looked at Jeffie with surprise. "You might say that it is. The word 'adopt' means to choose someone, and to bring them into your own family. Sure enough, that's what you did with Frosty, wasn't it?"

"I think *she* adopted *me*." Jeffie said with a giggle. "Because she chose first. But *now* I've adopted her, too. She's part of the family." He leaned down and scratched behind Frosty's left

14

ear. The cat purred even louder. "But adopting people is different from adopting cats and dogs. How did you and Daddy decide to adopt a little girl?"

Mom put aside her dish towel and sat down at the table. "Come sit by me," she told Jeffie. This was an important conversation. She wanted to make sure that he understood.

"After Morrie died," Mom began, "Daddy and I prayed a lot about having another baby someday." She gave Jeffie a hug. "We missed Morrie so much. Even though we still had you, the house seemed empty. We love children. And too, we wanted you to have a brother or sister."

Jeffie's eyes were sad. "I was lonesome too." He laid his head on the table and looked up at his mother.

"As Daddy and I prayed," Mom said, "we felt God was telling us to think about all the children who don't have homes. So we talked to a woman at an adoption agency who showed us pictures of boys and girls who need a family. Some are babies, and some are older than you are. These kids live with foster families or in orphanages." Mom's face looked sad. "They're growing older without the love of a forever

15

mommy and daddy. Children who grow up this way have a great sadness inside."

"What's a foster family?" Jeffie wanted to know. He tipped his cereal bowl and drank the last sip of milk.

"A foster family is a family who agrees to keep a homeless child, or maybe children who's parents can't take care of them or have hurt them. But foster families don't adopt.

"Sometimes the children stay only a few weeks. But even if they stay in the foster home for years, both the parents and children know that they'll probably leave someday. The child knows, too, that these aren't his real parents. Sometimes foster children go back to their own homes."

Jeffie looked puzzled. "I wouldn't want to be a foster child," he said, shaking his head.

"It's not necessarily a *bad* situation," Mom told him. "But everyone knows that it's not forever."

Just then Frosty jumped on the table. Jeffie picked her up and held her in his lap.

"An orphanage is a place where many home-less children live together," Mom went on. "Grown-ups watch over them and make sure they are fed and clothed. But often there isn't much time for story reading, singing, and cuddling together."

"Oh," said Jeffie. "I wouldn't like that."

"Well, since we wanted another child," Mom continued, "and since there are many children who need a family, it made sense to see if we could adopt one of them."

"How did you decide on Sandi?" Jeffie asked. "Did you just pick her out from a bunch of pictures?"

Mom laughed. "No," she said. "Mr. Feldon helped us. He's the social worker. Do you remember when he came here and talked to all of us and asked to look at the house? Before he let us take a child, he wanted to be sure that we will give it a good home."

"But our house is kind of old, and it isn't very big," Jeffie said, looking a little worried. Suddenly he began to wonder if their house was nice enough for Sandi. He thought about the pajamas that he'd left on the floor by his bed, too.

"Oh, Mr. Feldon wasn't looking for a big, beautiful house," Mom told him. "He was more interested in the family who lives inside. He was interested in us! He only looked around the house to make sure it was safe and that there was enough room for another child."

"Oh," said Jeffie. He looked at his mother with a grin. "Did he like us, then?"

"He said that our family was just right for Sandi," she said. "He told us that he'd been wondering who would be the best family to adopt her."

"I'm glad it's us," Jeffie said, giving a little bounce.

"Me, too."

Frosty jumped to the floor and walked to the kitchen door, her tail swishing. "She wants to go out," Mom chuckled. She got up and opened the door. Frosty dashed outside and up a tree.

Without being reminded, Jeffie took his dishes to the sink.

"You must remember," Mom said thoughtfully, "that Sandi has had a rough life for a 3-year-old. Her parents died, and she's been in several foster homes since then." She paused, watching Frosty rolling around in the grass. The cat had a good life. A better life than little Sandi had had so far.

"Not everyone Sandi stayed with was kind to her," Mom said softly. "Some of the foster mothers didn't have time to look after her. And Mr. Feldon told us that she hasn't been eating the right kind of food, either. Sandi may not look her best when she arrives. Frosty didn't, you know."

Jeffie looked down at the sleek white cat stretching in the sunshine. He thought of how it looked when it first came to their door. "I'll remember," he said. "And after Sandi gets used to us and eats the right kind of food for a while, she'll look better."

"That's right," Mom agreed. "But the thing that will change Sandi the most will be that her new family—that's us—love and accept her. If she knows we like her just the way she is, she'll become a beautiful child."

"It wasn't hard to like Frosty, even when she was all wet and raggedy," Jeffie said thoughtfully. "I liked her the minute I saw her. And I'll like Sandi, too. Having a real girl will be even nicer than having a cat. And I'll teach her to be nice to Frosty. They ought to understand each other pretty well because they'll *both* be adopted!"

Jeffie Gets Adopted Too

Chapter 2

"Is it worship time now, Mama?" asked Jeffie. "I'll get the storybook!"

He pulled the Bible storybook from the bookcase shelf. "Here it is," he said. "We're on the story of Baby Moses now."

"That's a good story for us to read today," said Mom, "because Moses was adopted by an Egyptian princess. Let's read about it."

Jeffie had never thought of Moses being adopted. He listened with more interest than usual. He began to wonder how it would feel to have to leave his family and go live with a heathen princess. "It's a wonder that Moses didn't become a heathen too," he told Mom.

"Oh, but Moses' mother taught him to worship the God of heaven," Mom answered. "She taught him carefully, for she knew he would leave her home one day. So even though his new family worshipped idols, he was always true to God."

Jeffie jumped up and ran to a bookcase. Soon he found a picture book about Egypt. Together he and Mom looked at pictures of Egyptian pyramids and some of the idols that the Egyptians worshipped. His finger traced a picture of a statue with the head of a cow.

"That's Hathor," Mom said. "And that's one of the idols that Moses could have been taught about."

"Wow!" Jeffie said. "But he didn't ever pray to it, did he? He only prayed to God."

"No," said Mom. "Moses had been taught when he was a child that these lifeless images weren't real gods."

Jeffie closed the book and hugged it to his chest. "The Bible has a lot of things in it. It has the same kind of things that happen today. I didn't know that people in olden times adopted children. Are there any more stories about adopted children in the Bible?"

"Oh, yes. The child Samuel was adopted. You remember that story, don't you?"

He nodded. "We had that story in church. Samuel's mom didn't have any babies for a long time. So she prayed, and then God gave her a boy. And she was so thankful that she gave him to God."

He wiggled around, scooting to the end of the sofa. "That doesn't make sense, Mama. If she wanted a baby so badly and prayed so hard, why did she give him away after she got him?"

"That's a good question," Mom said. "In Samuel's day, the firstborn son was always dedicated to God. That was to remind people that God's firstborn Son would one day be given to the world. So Samuel's mother was following their custom when she dedicated him to God."

"But why did she give him away?"

Mom looked thoughtful. "I believe Hannah knew that Samuel was a special child and would need training in God's house. She believed that God would use him to help the people of Israel. I think she missed him a lot, but she was willing to let Eli take him."

"She didn't forget him," added Jeffie. "Every year she brought him a little coat that she'd made. And I guess she prayed for him every single day."

"Did you ever wonder why God would put Samuel in Eli's home?" Mom asked. "Eli wasn't a good father, you know. His own sons were very wicked men."

"He probably never made them put their nose on the wall when they were naughty," said Jeffie, eyeing a certain corner of the room. "Or have a time-out on their bed."

"Maybe not," Mom agreed. "If Mr. Feldon had visited Eli before he adopted Samuel, he might have said, 'I'm sorry, Mr. Eli, but your home does not qualify for taking a child at this time.' But God knew what He was doing. He protected Samuel and helped him be a good boy." She smiled. "You know, God was really Samuel's Father. God began speaking to him and training him when Samuel was still a child."

"God is my Father, too," said Jeffie. "The Bible says so, doesn't it?"

Mom picked up the Bible and turned the pages before answering. Then she read, "Through Him we are born again, which makes God our Father. And what a kind and loving Father God is!" (Romans 8:16, Clear Word/Kids).

"Who wrote that?" Jeffie asked.

"Paul."

"Was Paul adopted, too?"

"Not that we know of," Mom answered. "But he was much like a son to his teacher Gamaliel. And later, when Paul became a Christian, he became like a father to Timothy. He called Timothy his son."

Jeffie jumped up again. It was hard to sit in one spot for so long. He squatted down, tucked his head, and did a somersault. His mom clapped, and he laughed. "Are there any stories in the Bible about adopted girls?" he asked.

"Yes," said Mother. "Esther was adopted by her cousin Mordecai."

Jeffie said, "I remember! Mordecai took her because her mother and father died." His eyes grew round with excitement. "Just like Sandi!" he said. "Her mother and father died, too."

Mom and Jeffie turned to the story of Esther in Jeffe's Bible picture book. "She became a queen," Jeffie said.

"All these adopted children in the Bible became important heroes for God," Mother pointed out. "God placed them in these homes for particular reasons. Moses became a great leader for his people. Samuel was Israel's most-loved prophet and judge. Esther saved all the Jewish people in Persia from death. The training they received in their adoptive homes helped prepare them for their life work for God."

Jeffie was thoughtful. "Do you think God is putting Sandi in our home," he asked, "so that she will get training to become a hero for God?"

"I'm sure of it!" Mother answered. "Each of us can be a hero for God, even if we never become famous." She turned a few pages of her Bible and read, "Because He loved us so, He decided to secure our future by adopting us as His children. This happened to His plan through Jesus" (Ephesians 1:5, Clear Word/Kids).

"Does that mean that Jesus has adopted *all* the children in the world?"

"No. It means He *wants* to adopt every person," Mom said. "But He won't *make* us be His children unless we want to be adopted."

"H'mm." Jeffie was thinking. "That's not how we're doing it with Sandi," he said after a moment. "She probably doesn't know very much about what is happening to her. And she didn't get to choose us."

"You're right," Mom agreed. "Sandi isn't

old enough to choose. People who care about Sandi are choosing for her."

"Who chooses when we're adopted by God?" Jeffie wanted to know.

"God chooses," Mom told him. "And people choose, too. People like you and me and Daddy. And Grandpa and Grammie—"

"And Tommy and Brad," Jeffie shouted happily, naming two friends who lived down the street.

"Yes," Mom said. "God cares enough so that He never *makes* us choose Him. He wants us to decide for ourselves."

"Then I want to be adopted, too," Jeffie said, "and grow up to be a hero for God. Can I do it right *now?* Am I old enough to choose?"

"You *can* do it right now!" Mother answered.

They folded their hands and bowed their heads while Jeffie prayed. "Dear Jesus," he said, "I'm big enough to choose now, and I want to be adopted by You. Please do it. Amen."

He looked up to see Mom wiping a tear from her eye. "Don't cry, Mom," he said. "Adoption is a happy thing. It makes me feel good inside. Now I'm part of God's family too."

Waiting for Sandi

Chapter 3

The weeks dragged by so slowly. Jeffie counted them by Sabbaths, because that was an easy way to remember.

"Only one more Sabbath," he said to Daddy one Friday afternoon. "Just think, after this Sabbath we can take Sandi to Sabbath school with us. Don't you think she'll look cute in the pretty yellow dress with the lace on the front that we bought for her?"

"Yes," said Daddy, "but I'm not sure how she'll act. Sandi has never been to church before."

The family was sitting around the dinner table. Jeffie had finished his roast and baked potato. Now he took a bite of a crisp carrot stick. But he frowned, thinking of his new sister acting up in church.

"Sometimes little children are frightened when they go to a new place," Mom said. "And I don't think that Sandi's foster parents took her to church. Probably no one has taught her to be quiet and reverent. When you were still a baby, Daddy and I taught you to fold your hands and bow your head for prayer. Sandi doesn't know things like that. So we'll have to be patient while she's learning."

Jeffie nodded. "Is there any way I can help?"

"Yes," said Daddy. "If you're reverent during prayer, and quiet during church, Sandi will learn by watching you how she should behave in church. It may take a few weeks, but she'll learn."

"And there's something else you can do to help," Mom added. "I'm going to make Sandi a Quiet Book to look at during the church service. You can help me cut out the pieces."

"Oh, good!" Jeffie cried. "I remember when I was little and had a Quiet Book. That was fun. I always liked zipping the zipper best of all. There was a picture under it. And I liked to button on the flowers. Can we make button-on flowers in Sandi's book?"

"Of course," Mom said with a big smile.

The next morning they had a good time cutting bright felt pieces and fitting them together for Sandi's Quiet Book. They couldn't finish it in one day but Jeffie was happy to see how much they got done. Working on the book seemed to make the time go faster.

"Mom," Jeffie asked a day or two later, "are we going to have a big party when Sandi comes?" His eyes were on the ball he was bouncing. He was counting the bounces in his head. But his voice asked, "Will we invite all our friends and relatives to meet her?"

Mom shook her head. "No, that would not be best for Sandi." She pulled on her gardening gloves. Then she knelt on a little mat before a bed of daisies and yellow zinnias and began snipping off dead flower heads.

Jeffie felt disappointed, but Mom explained. "We feel like we know Sandi because we've seen her picture and we've waited a long time to meet her. But we're strangers to her, you know. She's so young that she may not even understand that she's going to stay with us always."

Jeffie hadn't thought about that. Somehow he'd expected that Sandi would be as excited to meet her new big brother as he was to meet her. Now he wondered if she'd miss her foster family. Maybe there'd been other kids to play with there. Even though Mom had said she hadn't always had good food, maybe she liked that food. A shiver ran down his back. He'd be scared if someone picked him up and took *him* to a family he'd never met before.

His mother's voice brought him back to the front yard where she was pulling weeds from around the flowers. "In fact," Mom said, turning to look at Jeffie, "we'll ask our friends not to come for a few days. They'll need to wait until Sandi is rested and feels comfortable here. Then we can have Grammie and Grandpa over. A lot of people will want to see Sandi, but we must think of how she might feel."

Jeffie started slowly bouncing the ball again—one, two, three, four. He grabbed it on the fifth bounce. Things seemed to be getting complicated.

"Will I get to go to the airport when you and Daddy go to get her?" he asked slowly.

"Oh, yes!" Mom answered. "We want Sandi

to meet her new brother right away. After all, you're showing your love for her by sharing your mommy and daddy. Adoption is sharing, too, Jeffie."

Jeffie gave a big sigh of happiness. He felt so good he threw the ball as high as he could, and ran to be under it when it came down. Then with a great big jump, he caught it.

———

It didn't seem like it would ever come, but one morning Jeffie woke while it was still dark. He lay in bed thinking, *Today is THE DAY!* Today they would drive to the airport and meet Sandi.

Jeffie snuggled in bed until he heard Frosty mew outside his door. He got up to let her in. Frosty cuddled next to him while he told the cat all about Sandi. "And you'll be her—" He tried to think what relation Frosty would be to Sandi. Finally he decided that Frosty would be called "an adopted girl's adopted cat." Just then Mom came to the door.

"I'm already up!" Jeffie cried, jumping out of bed. "I was awake a long time ago. What shall I wear?"

"Wear everyday clothes," Mom told him.

"We want Sandi to see us the way we usually are. She isn't used to seeing people dressed up in suits and special dresses."

So Jeffie put on clean jeans and a blue T-shirt. He found matching socks and slipped on his tennies. While he dressed, he was thinking about something important.

"Mom," he said, as he came into the kitchen, "you said that when God adopts us, it's a lot like when we adopt someone. Now we're going to meet Sandi for the first time and we're just wearing our ordinary clothes. Is *that* the same as what God did?"

Mom smiled and nodded. "Yes," she said. "You're a smart boy to think of that, too. Jesus had to come down to earth to start working on our adoption. And the first time anybody saw Him, what did He look like?"

Jeffie thought a minute. "Just like a regular baby, I guess."

"You're right." She put cinnamon-raisin bread in the toaster then went to the fridge for blueberries.

"Jesus could have dressed up in His best and brightest glory," she said. "In fact, that's what the Jews thought He would do. But instead He came dressed in an ordinary human body. He wanted people to love Him just for Himself, and not because He was rich, beautiful, and glorious looking."

"Just like we'll love Sandi for herself, and not because she's pretty?" Jeffie asked.

"That's right," said Daddy, as he came into the kitchen buttoning the last button in his shirt. "And do you know, when we love Sandi, Jesus counts it as if we were loving Him."

"Really?" Jeffie asked. That was an interesting thought. "How does that work, Daddy?"

"When Jesus comes again," Daddy explained, "He will say to His children who love Him, 'Thank you for feeding Me when I was hungry. And thank you for giving Me clothes when I didn't have any. And thank you for visiting Me when I was sick and when I was in prison. And thank you for taking Me into your home.' Then the good people will say, 'Why, Jesus! When did we ever see *You* hungry or sick? When did we give *You* food and clothes and a home?' And Jesus will say, 'Whatever you did to My little children, you have done to Me.'"

"Wow, Daddy!" Jeffie exclaimed. "I always

did want to do something wonderful for Jesus. And now I can."

Mom nodded. "That's true. By giving Sandi a home, we give Jesus a home too."

Sandi Comes Home

Chapter 4

W aiting for this airplane is so exciting," Jeffie said, hopping on one foot and then the other. "Just think, we get to meet Sandi *for real* today. I think," he said thoughtfully, "it's a little like waiting for Jesus to come."

He pressed his face against the big glass window. A silver jet was coming down from the sky. "Is that the plane?" he asked.

"I don't think so," Daddy said. "It's still 10 minutes until Sandi's plane is due."

"Is *that* the plane?" Jeffie asked a few minutes later.

"No," said Mom. "That's the wrong airline. Sandi's plane is due at 10:05, and her plane will be yellow with a red stripe going down the side. If we go meet the wrong plane, we won't find Sandi on it."

"We must wait for the right plane if we want to see Sandi," said Daddy, "just as we must look for the right signs when Jesus comes. Satan will try to trick us by making it look as if Jesus is in this place or that place on the earth. But the Bible says He will come in the clouds and *everyone* will see Him."

Jeffie tried to wait patiently for the right plane, but he just couldn't be still. His whole body wanted to wiggle. He was so excited. Then a few minutes later Daddy said, "It's 10:03. The plane should be very close."

Jeffie jumped up and down, hoping that would help him see better. Then suddenly he called, "Mommy! Daddy! I see it!" He grabbed Daddy's hand. "See, way over there? It's a yellow plane." Jeffie's heart thumped with excitement. Now, at last! Soon he'd see Sandi.

"This is where the passengers come from the plane," Daddy told him as they walked toward a long ramp. "Watch for Mr. Feldon. He'll be carrying Sandi. Look! There he is now. See, Jeffie. Here's your new sister!"

Mr. Feldon smiled as he came up the ramp. "Well, folks, here she is," he said as he placed a thin, small brown-haired girl in Mother's arms. Mom began to cry. Daddy smiled. Sandi yawned.

"She just woke up," Mr. Feldon explained. "She had a very good trip. Can you see her, Jeffie?"

Jeffie had been standing on tiptoe, trying to get a look at Sandi's face. But as Sandi woke up a little more and realized that she was the center of attention, she buried her face in Mom's shoulder.

"I can't see her very well," said Jeffie. "She's kind of shy, I guess." He looked at Sandi's back. She was smaller than he'd expected. Her legs stuck out like thin sticks from under her dress. Her skin was very pale.

"Let's get these papers signed," suggested Mr. Feldon. "Then you folks can take Sandi to the restroom and get on home. She hasn't been feeling well the last few days, and the sooner she can get to a quiet place, the better it will be for her."

Suddenly Jeffie felt worried. Was Sandi sick? Did that mean she wouldn't want to play with him? He knew to expect her to be shy, but he hadn't thought she could be sick. His own tummy didn't feel so good as he thought about his new sister. He turned to watch as Mr. Feldon took out some papers and a pen and Mommy and Daddy wrote their names underneath all the printing.

"What does that say?" Jeffie asked.

Mr. Feldon patted his shoulder. "It says that your family has received one little 3-year-old girl named Sandi, and that she will now be living in your home," he answered with a smile.

Sandi was very quiet on the way home. Jeffie began to wonder if she knew how to talk. He handed her the little brown-haired doll. She took it, but did not speak. Strapped in her car seat, she didn't make a sound. But Jeffie saw that her eyes darted back and forth and sometimes her lip trembled.

It seemed to take a long time to get home. Mom sang some Sabbath school songs and now and then turned around to smile at Sandi. At last Daddy pulled into the driveway. Mom lifted Sandi out of the car seat and carried her into the house. She still hadn't said one word.

Then she saw a large bowl of plastic fruit on

the coffee table. Her eyes opened wide.

"Food!" Sandi cried. "Want food!"

"She can talk," Jeffie said excitedly. "Look, Mom. She wants to eat the plastic fruit."

Mom laughed softly, while Daddy reached over and took a real banana from a bowl on the kitchen counter. He peeled it and gave a piece to Sandi. "Here, little one," he said. "This will be better for you than plastic fruit."

Sandi eagerly grabbed the piece of banana and put it in her mouth.

Jeffie looked seriously at his father. "Daddy," he said, "you just gave a banana to Jesus."

Mrs. Fitzgerald's Visit

Chapter 5

The rest of the day passed quickly. Jeffie tried to be quiet and let Sandi adjust. But inside, he was still excited as could be. He had a new sister! Perhaps it was because he had *not* been able to run and shout and tell everybody at the top of his voice, that he said what he did to Mrs. Fitzgerald.

Yes, she came. No one had thought to tell Mrs. Fitzgerald to wait a few days. Just at dusk Jeffie looked out the window and groaned. "Oh, no," he said. "There's Mrs. Fitzgerald's blue car."

Mom looked a little troubled, but said,

"Don't worry, Jeffie. She usually doesn't stay too long. Daddy and I will talk with her a bit."

A firm rapping sounded at the door, and Mom opened it. "Hello, Mrs. Fitzgerald," she said. "Won't you come in for a few minutes?"

Mrs. Fitzgerald walked in. She saw Sandi. And right away she said just the wrong thing.

"Why, my dear!" she exclaimed in her loud, high voice. "Is this the little girl you are *adopting?*"

"Yes, it is," answered Mom pleasantly. "And we're being very quiet today, because she is still adjusting."

Mrs. Fitzgerald didn't seem to understand that Mom was asking her to speak more quietly. She went on in an excited voice, "She—she doesn't look too healthy. Are you *sure* you want to take in a waif like this? There may be something wrong with her, you know. And surely one wouldn't want to expose a nice little boy like *Jeffie* to some *dangerous disease.*"

Mom was about to reply, but Jeffie could keep still no longer. His eyes were bright with tears of anger.

"There's nothing dangerous about Sandi," he said in a shaky voice. "And even if there *was* something wrong with her, we'd still want her.

Because adoption is when you see that something is wrong, and you try to make it right. And besides, adopting somebody is caring about how they feel. And it is loving little kids that don't have their own mommies and daddies. And it's sharing homes with kids that—" All of Jeffie's excitement and anger burst into big teardrops that rolled down his cheeks.

The shiny stones on Mrs. Fitzgerald's dress flashed and sparkled when she breathed hard, as she was doing now. But in a moment she got control of herself. In a kinder voice she said, "Of course, Jeffie. I didn't mean to upset you." She paused and then added, "Perhaps this little girl only needs plenty of food, and a nice family like yours."

Jeffie gulped a few times, wiped his face on his sleeve, and nodded. Mom and Daddy started talking then, and Jeffie sneaked out. He went to his bedroom, shut the door, and cried a little more. He lay quietly on his bed listening to the grown-ups' voices in the next room until he fell asleep.

When he awoke, it was dark. Mrs. Fitzgerald had gone. He got up and made his way to the living room. "I'm sorry," he mumbled, "for saying all that stuff to Mrs. Fitzgerald. She doesn't know what adopting is about. She called Sandi 'dangerous.'"

"Well," said Mom, bending down to give him a hug. "Perhaps you were a bit excited. But we did have a wonderful visit after things settled down."

"What did she say?"

"Well, she began to see that we weren't taking Sandi because it was a nice thing to do, but because we really want her to be a part of our family. She was sorry that she spoke without thinking. But the best part was that Daddy and I were able to talk to her about how God has adopted us into His family.

"You know, Jeffie, as we talked, she looked at Sandi all the time. And once she even got tears in her eyes."

"Tears in her eyes?" he asked, surprised. "Real tears?"

"I saw them, Jeffie. And I have a feeling—" Mom stopped talking and gave a happy laugh. "I just have a great big wonderful feeling that someday Mrs. Fitzgerald is going to let God adopt *her.*"

"That would be great," Jeffie said. "Then

she'd know how we feel about Sandi." He looked around the room. "How is Sandi, Mom? Where is she?"

"She's all right. The visit didn't seem to bother her too much. She's in bed in her new fuzzy pink pajamas. Would you like to go in and see her?"

Jeffie and Mommy tiptoed into the bedroom where a night light glowed softly near Sandi's bed. She was snuggled down under the new patch-work quilt, sucking her thumb. Jeffie thought she was sleeping. But when he came near she opened her eyes and said sleepily, "Hi, Deffie."

"Hi, Sandi," he whispered, grinning at the way she said his name. He gently patted her hair. "You be a good girl and go to sleep now. Everything's going to be all right."

Sandi's First Sabbath

Chapter 6

Sandi had arrived on a Tuesday. Just four days later she spent her first Sabbath in her new home.

"I wonder what she thinks about today," Jeffie said Friday morning. "She can see we're busier today."

"We can't tell what she thinks, but we can teach her about Sabbath," Mom said. "One of the best ways to teach small children, Jeffie, is to sing to them. Do you remember some of the songs you sang in beginners?"

It seemed like a very long time ago that *he* was only 3, but Jeffie did remember one of his favorite songs, "Sabbath Is a Happy Day." So he began to sing it to Sandi. Perhaps no one had ever sung to Sandi before because she seemed very curious about how he made this new sound. Walking up to him, she tried to look inside his mouth and down his throat to see where it came from. This made Jeffie giggle.

But he grew serious. He realized that Sandi had never heard the happy songs he'd grown up with. He wanted to teach her as many as he could.

"Here, Sandi," he said, "this one you have to clap to." And he took her small hands in his own and made them pat together. At that, she got very excited and made high sounds.

"See, Mom! It's her first time," Jeffie cried. "She's already trying to sing. She'll probably be a good singer some day!"

Jeffie did his chores as fast as he could that afternoon, so he could spend more time with Sandi after her nap. He showed her pictures of Jesus, and had her sit on a small chair to listen just as she'd do in Sabbath school.

"Just imagine," he told Daddy that evening. "She's 3 years old and never been to Sabbath school before."

"Yes," said Daddy. "There are many people much older than Sandi who have never heard of the Sabbath." He smiled. "In fact, some of them will be in heaven." Daddy was helping Jeffie put away his toys that Sandi had left on the floor. Sandi was in the kitchen watching Mom fix dinner.

Jeffie was surprised at what Daddy said. "I thought that if people don't keep all God's commandments, they won't get to heaven," he told Daddy.

"The Bible says that God has children from all nations," Daddy told him. "And we're told that those who have no Bibles, but are loving and kind are God's true children also. Even though they've never heard of Jesus, they have listened and obeyed His Holy Spirit." Jeffie put a red truck and a stuffed tiger in the toy box, and Daddy closed the lid.

"Some people have never heard of God's true Sabbath," Daddy said. "When they get to heaven, Jesus Himself will teach them."

"Wow! That's what I'm doing with Sandi," said Jeffie.

"I know," Daddy nodded. "I'm glad. She really needs a big brother to help her learn some of these things. It will be a help to Mama and me."

Sabbath morning Jeffie woke up early and looked out the window. It was a perfect day to be Sandi's first Sabbath. The sun was already drying the dew from the grass and a gentle breeze was blowing. He pulled the covers up on his bed then went to help Sandi. She was sitting on the floor by the window, playing with her new toys.

"Not today, Sandi," said Jeffie gently taking the toys and putting them on a shelf. "We have special toys for today—Sabbath toys."

Sandi's lips turned down as if she was going to cry. "It's OK," Jeffie said quickly. He opened the box he'd taken from the closet. In it were Bible picture books, a doctor and nurse kit, and a felt board with felt animal pieces. "See? These are Sabbath toys," he said, showing them to his little sister. "We'll play with them after church today. You can be the missionary nurse. But now, you have to eat breakfast. Want to eat, Sandi?"

She nodded, still looking at the toys.

"Come on," Jeffie said. "I bet you're hungry."

So Sandi followed him into the kitchen and watched as he looked in the cupboard. Mom always kept granola and fruit in one cupboard for breakfast. He looked at the cereal and frowned. He didn't think Sandi's teeth were strong enough to chew granola. "Want a banana?" he asked her. He sliced a banana and they each ate the pieces one at a time.

When Mom came into the kitchen he asked, "What shall Sandi eat?"

"I have some puffed wheat," she answered, handing him a bowl. "Would you like to fix it for her?"

Jeffie put some cereal and milk in the bowl. Then he helped Sandi to fold her hands and say, "Thank You, Jesus."

After breakfast everyone hurried to get ready. Daddy had said it might be best if they got to church early. Soon Jeffie, Mommy, Daddy, and Sandi were ready. Sandi, wearing her pretty yellow dress, looked wide-eyed at everything. "Sabbath is a happy day, happy day, happy day . . . ," Jeffie sang and Mom and Daddy joined in as they drove to church. A new church bag rested on the seat beside them. Inside was the Quiet Book, all finished and ready for Sandi to enjoy.

"I'll stay with Sandi in beginners," Mama said. "We don't know how she'll react to Sabbath school."

Of course, many people stopped them to see Sandi and to ask how she was doing. The greeter put a red rose sticker on Sandi's dress, but she pulled it off and tried to eat it. Mother had to take it from her.

The Beginners leader was happy to meet Sandi, too. She pinned a little felt puppy on her dress. Sandi tried to pull that off, too, and almost tore her dress. So she went without a name tag.

"When the singing started," Mom told Jeffie and Daddy, later, "Sandi was as good as gold. She loved keeping time with the sticks and bells. She liked putting felt pictures on the board. At first she wanted to keep all the things the teacher gave her, but soon she began to catch on that she was supposed to give them back after each song."

By the time church started, Sandi was tired. After looking around at all the people, she buried her head in Mom's shoulder. The next time Jeffie looked at her, she'd fallen asleep.

"She didn't get to use her Quiet Book," he whispered, disappointed.

"No, she didn't," said Mom quietly. "But there will be many other Sabbaths."

And there were. Sandi grew to love Sabbath

school very much, just as Jeffie had hoped she would. And not too long after Sandi started going to Sabbath school, someone else did, too. It was Mrs. Fitzgerald.

Week after week, she came to church. And week by week Jeffie saw that she was learning about Jesus, just as Sandi was. He began to look forward to Mrs. Fitzgerald's visits. She was different, somehow.

Jeffie thought about it. But Sandi was different, too.

So he asked his mom how this happened. "Learning about Jesus changes people," she told him. She smiled, and winked at him. "I know someone else who's changed a lot in the past few weeks, too."

Jeffie grinned a little. "Yes, I know," he said. "It's me! I've learned more about Jesus, and I'm different too."

Jeffie's Real Sister

Chapter 7

The warm days of summer brought many changes to Jeffie's family. Jeffie had a birthday. Now he was 7. Sandi grew healthy and strong. She loved to play in the small yard with Frosty. The cat seemed to know they had something in common. She never tried to scratch or bite, even when Sandi's play was rough. And as time went on, Sandi learned to be kind to Frosty.

Mrs. Fitzgerald came over more often. Jeffie liked to talk with her now. He noticed that she took a special interest in Sandi for she often brought her small presents.

Once, she brought candy. Mom gave her a little hug and said, "Oh, I'm sorry, but I can't give her that." Mrs. Fitzgerald looked surprised but Mom explained why.

"You know, she was not well when she came. I don't think she'd ever eaten right. So we're trying to feed her only the best food. We want her to be healthy."

"Oh, of course. I hadn't thought of that," Mrs. Fitzgerald quickly said. "I'm not around little children very often. Of course you wouldn't want to give her candy. It might—" She thought a moment. "It might give her cavities. And we wouldn't want such a pretty little girl to have ugly rotten teeth, would we Jeffie?"

"Nope," Jeffie agreed.

As the weeks passed Sandi's dull, thin hair became shiny. Her skin took on a warm, rosy glow, and she started growing. Before summer was over, Mama gave the pretty yellow dress to another little girl. It was too small for Sandi.

But Jeffie thought the best day that summer was when the real estate man came to look at the house. They were going to move out of town. Soon Jeffie and Sandi would live in the country. There they might even have a pony.

Mr. White, the real estate man, looked all over their house. He walked around the yard. He talked to Daddy about improvements, and paint, and landscaping. Jeffie didn't understand all they said. But he would never forget the last thing Mr. White said.

As he was getting ready to leave, Jeffie took Sandi in his arms and stood by Mr. White's car. "Hello there, young man," said the real estate agent. "I guess I missed talking to you. How are you?"

"I'm fine," answered Jeffie politely. He looked proudly at Sandi and began, "And this is—"

He was going to say, "This is my little sister." But Mr. White cut in with a big laugh. "That's your little sister, right?"

Jeffie was pleased and surprised. "How did you know?" he asked.

"Easy," said Mr. White, smiling. "There's a definite family resemblance."

"What does that mean?" Jeffie asked.

"It means you and she look alike—like brother and sister," Mr. White said, as he started the car. "Cute little cricket, isn't she?" He laughed again, and reached out the window to give Sandi's cheek a gentle pat. "Well, see you folks later," he called as he drove away.

"Mom!" Jeffie called. "Mr. White said that Sandi and I look alike. How could he say that? I have blond hair and blue eyes. Sandi has brown hair and brown eyes, and she's a lot thinner than I am. How could he say we look alike?"

Mom smiled. "I'll tell you about it at worship tonight. But, you know what? I agree with him. You *do* look alike. Maybe your colors aren't the same, but there's something else that makes people know right away that you are brother and sister.

"What is it?" Jeffie asked with great curiosity.

"I don't know exactly what it's called," Mom admitted. "Maybe it has something to do with the way Sandi and you act and talk. She copies you a lot and it makes her seem like your real sister."

"She *is* my real sister," said Jeffie proudly.

———◆———

"Now, Mom," Jeffie reminded her at family worship, "you said you were going to tell me about having a family re-remem—rebemlance. Oh, what's that word Mr. White used?"

"'Resemblance,'" she answered. "He said

55

there was a family resemblance between you and Sandi. Did you know that the same thing happens when God adopts us as His children? As we think about Him and learn His ways, we begin to act like Him. We begin to look different."

"Oh, yes. I know what you mean," said Jeffie. "Remember once, when you were in the store and that woman behind you leaned over and poked you with her elbow. She said, 'Excuse me, but you're a Christian, aren't you?' I always wondered how she could tell."

"It's because when we study Jesus' life and think about Him, we begin to act like Him," Mom said.

"I remember when we were at Morrie's funeral," Jeffie said thoughtfully, "and I thought some of the people there weren't church people. How did I know that?" he asked himself. "Let's see. Some smelled funny, like cigarettes. And when I stepped on a man's foot, by accident, he said a bad word."

"You must understand, Jeffie," said Daddy, "that even people like that may be Christians. Perhaps they've just learned about Jesus, and don't fully understand how His love works in their hearts. If you were to see them a few years later, it might be easier to know they are Christians. They would have had time to grow more like Jesus."

"I think," said Jeffie, "that Christians look kinder. If they've had time to learn about Jesus," he added quickly. "I hope," he said thoughtfully, "that everybody that sees us can tell we belong to God's family, the same as Mr. White could tell that Sandi belongs to ours."

Mother said, "Let's ask Jesus to make it so."

Moving Closer to Heaven

Chapter 8

W ell," Daddy said one evening as he got home from work, "we have a buyer for the house." He looked especially happy. "That means we can move out to that little farm we've been looking at, just outside of town."

"Yippee!" Jeffie hollered, and jumped up in the air. "Sandi! Sandi!" he called. "We get to move to the country. And we can have a pony all for ourselves."

"A pony?" She sounded puzzled.

"It's like a little horse. I'll teach you how to ride," he promised.

"Wide?" asked Sandi. She'd never been near

a real pony before.

"*Rrrr-ide.* Say, *rrrr,*" Jeffie told her.

"*Rrrr,*" said Sandi.

"Good," said Jeffie. "I'm going to teach you how to *rrr-ide* the pony, when we get him. And we can have a little garden, with corn and peas and carrots and lettuce. Won't that be fun? I'll show you how to dig. We'll get you a little shovel."

"Shub-o?" said Sandi.

"Oh, you're so cute," Jeffie laughed, giving her a hug. "Yes, a real shovel, all for you. Come in my room and I'll show you what a shovel is." He got the farm picture book Daddy had bought them, and showed her a picture of a shovel leaning up against a barn. "Shovel," said Jeffie. "And besides the garden, there's a big tree out there."

He took Sandi's hand and led her to the living room, saying, "Daddy said he'd put up a swing for us—didn't you, Dad?" Their father looked up from sorting the mail, smiling at Jeffie's enthusiasm as he told Sandi, "I'll show you how to pump and get it swinging, so when I'm at school you can swing by yourself."

Daddy picked up Sandi and set her on his

lap. "Yes, we'll get a swing up, the first thing," he told the little girl. "Jeffie is so excited, you'd think we were going to heaven instead of just a few miles out of town."

"Daddy, do you suppose Jesus is just as excited about us moving to heaven as we are about moving to the country?" Jeffie asked seriously.

"I think He's even more excited," Daddy answered. "He has our gardens ready. The houses are all built. Maybe He's even put up some swings and slides for His littlest children. There are a lot of things in heaven that we've never seen before."

"Do you know about any of them?" Jeffie asked.

"The Bible tells us about some of them," his father said. "But the very best thing about being in heaven is that Jesus will be there."

Jeffie nodded. "Yeah, and He'll show us all the new stuff."

Daddy bounced Sandi on his lap. "Heaven will be even better than moving to the country, but living in the country will be lots of fun."

"I can hardly wait to get to heaven," Jeffie said. "I wish we were going there now, instead of just moving to the country."

With one arm Daddy pulled his son next to

him. "Moving to the country is a step toward moving to heaven," he said. "The air is cleaner. Instead of having houses and stores around us, we'll have trees and fields. And one thing I really like is seeing all the stars at night. Living here in town, we don't see many stars because of the lights. But out there I'm pretty sure we'll see the Milky Way."

"Really and truly?" Jeffie asked.

"Really and truly." Sandi was wiggling to get away so Daddy put her down. She plopped to the floor and leaned against his legs. "There's something else," Daddy said. "Something important."

"What?" That was Sandi's little voice.

"In the quietness of the country I think you can hear Jesus' voice in your heart more clearly."

"Then I'm glad we're moving *now*," Jeffie said, "so we can get more ready for Jesus. I want to see all the new things He has for us on our farm in heaven. Don't you, Sandi?"

And Sandi said, "Mmm-hmmm, Deffie. Me, too!

Sandi Gets Lost

Chapter 9

Moving day came at last. Jeffie was in school, so he missed some of the excitement. It was hard to keep his mind on his lessons though. He kept thinking of the moving truck being unloaded and of the new room he'd be sleeping in that night. As soon as the last bell rang he shot out the door. Mom was waiting for him in the car. It was too far to walk home now, so every day she'd take him to school and pick him up. He opened the door and saw Sandi sleeping in her car seat in the back.

"She's just worn out," Mom said. "Everything was new and exciting to her. She kept going around the house calling, 'Deffie, rrr–ide? Shub-o? Deffie?' and wondering where you were."

"Is everything moved?" Jeffie asked as he buckled his seat belt.

"Everything's off the truck," Mom sighed. "But it will be a while before everything is put away."

As the car pulled away from school Jeffie asked, "When can we get our pony?"

"I'm afraid that the pony will have to wait for a few weeks. Daddy must build a corral for it first. But we can have a small fall garden if you want."

"That would be OK," Jeffie said. He felt a little sad that he had to wait for the pony. "Can I help choose what we plant?"

"Of course." Mom seemed to know how he felt. "And you'll see. The time will pass very quickly. You'll have the pony before long."

Their car sped past the street where they used to live and Jeffie gave a little wave. Mom saw him and smiled. "I need to tell you something," she said. "Try to be especially patient with Sandi for a while. She's been moved around so much in her little lifetime that moving could be upsetting for her. She may be afraid that she'll lose her family again."

"I'll be careful with her," Jeffie assured Mom.

As they drove along, Mom said, "Jesus is thoughtful of us, just as we're trying to be thoughtful of Sandi. Just before we move to heaven, there will be a hard time, called the Time of Trouble. There will be a lot of natural disasters, and violence among people. Jesus knew this would be frightening for His children, so He told us about it ahead of time. He said, 'Don't be afraid. I will be with you through this hard time. It will not last long. Just trust Me. Soon I will come to take you home in the clouds.'"

"I'm glad He told us," Jeffie said. "If He hadn't, I might be afraid."

They came in sight of the farm just then and Jeffie leaned forward. "It's just like I remembered it," he said. "Only now *our* furniture and things are there, instead of the other people's. It looks more like home. Look! Daddy already put up the swing!"

"Yes, he said he would do that first, so you would have something to do while we are getting everything in place. Some of the rooms have to be painted before we can move the furniture in. You'll have to watch Sandi for us while we work."

The car bumping down the graveled driveway woke Sandi. Jeffie helped her out of the car seat and they went into the house. Mom helped Sandi put on her play overalls and Jeffie took her out to the swing. It wasn't long before he gave up trying to teach her to pump. Her legs just couldn't do it. So he pushed the swing for a while, and then took her to the sandpile. She started digging with an old spoon and pail, so he went to explore.

He wondered where he and Mom would have their garden. Then he saw a stone wall nearby, so he climbed over it and began to look around. It seemed like just a few minutes, but when he came back to the sand pile, Sandi was gone.

Jeffie's heart thumped hard. *Where is she?* he wondered. He ran and looked in the house, but she wasn't there. He looked around the big yard. There was no place for a little girl to hide. Were there any ponds or deep holes she could fall into? Could she get to the road? He didn't know. Tears filled his eyes as he did the only thing he knew to do. He knelt down in the sand pile and prayed.

"Dear Jesus, I'm sorry I forgot to watch Sandi. Please help me find her." He stayed on his knees for a moment trying to listen to Jesus. *Where would a little girl go?* As he knelt there, a great feeling of quietness came over him. He knew that Sandi was nearby. Then, opening his eyes, he saw the toolshed. He jumped up and raced to its open door.

There stood Sandi in the dusty, musty shed, tugging at a large spade.

"Shub-o. Shub-o, Deffie," she said happily.

Jeffie took the shovel and leaned it against the wall. Then he took her hand and tried to lead her away. She didn't want to go. "Nice little house, Deffie," she said.

Jeffie felt cross. "It's not a little house, Sandi. It's a dirty old toolshed. There might be things in here that could hurt you. Look, you've got spiderwebs in your hair. This isn't a good place to play. Maybe later Daddy will build you a playhouse."

He led her out of the shed. Now he didn't feel cross anymore. He just felt happy that she was found. "I thought you were lost," he told her. "But I prayed to Jesus, and He helped me find you."

They played by the swing until the sun was low in the sky. Jeffie pushed Sandi, then she tried to push him. They both laughed, and he held her on his lap and they swung together. Then they heard Mom's voice. "Jeffie! Sandi!" she called. "Come on in and wash up. It's time to eat."

The Fence

Chapter 10

The supper dishes had been cleared away, and Mom hung up her apron with a sigh. Daddy was in the living room looking through a moving box.

"I'm just going to relax this evening. The rest of the cleaning can wait until tomorrow," Mom said to Jeffie as she came into the living room. "We got a lot of work done today." She picked up a round frame with cloth stretched across it. A picture was printed on the cloth. Mom was filling in the lines of the picture with colored thread. She picked up a needle threaded with blue and began to work on a flower.

Sandi sat quietly looking at picture books and soon began to rub her eyes. *It was a big day for her, too,* Jeffie thought. He wondered if she'd been afraid in the shed without him. Maybe she didn't even know she was lost.

"Mom," he said, "Sandi got lost today for a little while. I was looking for a garden place, and I forgot about her. When I went back to the sandpile, she wasn't there." He took a deep breath. "I was scared. I didn't know if there was a pond around, or if she might go out to the road."

"I guess you were scared!" Mom said. "But the yard is all fenced, and there are no ponds."

"I was real scared," Jeffie admitted, "so I prayed, and Jesus helped me find her."

"Where was she?"

"In the toolshed. She thought it was a little house." He shook his head, laughing now that his sister was safely with them. "She found an old shovel in there and she wanted to dig. I was so glad to see her. But while I was looking for her, I remembered how the Good Shepherd went hunting for His lost sheep. And then I knew Jesus would help me find my lost girl."

Daddy stood up. "Would you like for me to read the story of the lost sheep for evening worship?"

So Daddy read the story, and Jeffie understood it better than before. "I'm glad the lost sheep got found," he said. "It's too bad they didn't have a fence around the pasture, like we have a fence around our farm."

"You're right," Daddy said. "But this story has another meaning, too. Jesus wants us to understand that *we* are like sheep. And God has put a kind of fence around us, too."

"What kind of fence is it, Daddy?" Jeffie asked.

"It's a ten-commandment fence," Daddy said.

"And it's built around our hearts," Mama added.

Daddy nodded. "That's right. When we start to think or do something that would hurt us, the ten-commandment fence reminds us, 'Thou shalt not.' If we obey and stay inside the fence, we save ourselves a lot of trouble. But if we break through the fence and wander away, we become lost sheep. Then Jesus must go out and search for us and bring us back."

"Do you know who is waiting outside the fence?" Mother asked.

Jeffie shook his head.

"It's Satan. The Bible says that he prowls

around like a roaring lion, waiting for those who disobey, so he can get them into even more trouble!"

Sandi looked up at that, and Mama held out her arms. The sleepy little girl crawled into her lap.

"You see," Daddy said, "Jesus wants His children to be as safe as possible, just as Mama and I want our children to be safe. One of the reasons we bought this farm is that it is completely fenced. It's a place where you can play safely." He looked at his son. "Jeffie, you are big enough to climb over the fence. But we are asking you not to. If you obey us, it will be easy for you to obey Jesus as you get older. And," he added with a smile, "Sandi will do as you do."

Jeffie smiled at Sandi. She returned his smile; then she slid to the floor and crawled to where he sat.

"When Jesus came to earth, He stayed inside the ten-commandment fence," Daddy said. "Jesus showed us the best way to live. He's an older brother to us, just as you are to Sandi. We are to copy Him, as Sandi copies you.

"God the Father was pleased with Jesus for being an obedient older brother. He knew that people would see and study how Jesus did things, and would follow His example."

"I want to do that," said Jeffie.

He gave Sandi a hug. "I'm so glad we adopted you," he said. "It helps me understand how Jesus felt when He adopted us. And besides, you're a sweet little girl."

Sandi gave Jeffie a big, wet kiss. "Deffie nice boy," she lisped. "Sandi wuv Deffie!"

"Jeffie loves Sandi, too," he whispered.

He looked up, his face shining. "Mom, do you know what? People who don't know about adopting are sure missing a lot. Adoption is one of the happiest things in the world."

Jesus Has the Last Word

Chapter 11

Summer ended. Fall came, and Jeffie and Sandi watched the leaves drop from the tree where Daddy had hung the swing. One morning the bare limbs were covered with white. It was the first snow Sandi had ever seen. Jeffie showed her how to make snow angels, and pulled her around on the sled.

Winter passed. Spring flowers came and went. There was one spot in the garden that puzzled Jeffie, because a lot of tall green leaves grew there. "Where are the flowers?" he asked Mom. She just smiled and said, "Wait and see."

Every day Jeffie looked at these plants. As the

summer days came, the beautiful leaves wilted to the ground. They turned dry and brown. Jeffie had watched every day, but there were no flowers. Now the plants were dead. After awhile, he forgot about them.

"Mom," he said one morning in late summer, "Sandi came to live with us just around summertime."

"Yes, it's been over a year since she arrived," Mom answered. "Can you see how much she has changed?" Sandi was 4 years old now.

They watched his little sister climb the corral fence with some grass for Charley, the pony. Her shiny hair fell around her shoulders. She leaned forward with her hand outstretched. "Here, Charley!" she called in a clear voice. "Come get the nice grass."

Charley trotted to the fence and *whuffled* around Sandi's hand, blowing most of the grass away. "Oh, Charley," scolded Sandi. "Don't blow. Now it's all fallen down." She climbed down and went to pick more grass.

Jeffie giggled at Sandi's trials with Charley. But he had a deep feeling of happiness as he watched her run across the yard on sturdy legs, her long, shiny hair blowing in the breeze.

But his smile faded as he thought of the brother he used to have. "Morrie would be about this old now, wouldn't he, Mama, if he was still alive?" And it surprised Jeffie that both of them started to cry. He hadn't cried for Morrie for a long time. But suddenly the sadness was there.

Mama held out her arms, and Jeffie scooted near to her. They hugged each other for a long time as they watched Sandi picking grass for the pony. When Jeffie could talk again, he said, "Mama, I want to take Sandi to see Morrie's grave. Will you take us today?"

"Yes," she said. "We have no special plans this morning. Let's go now."

So they called Sandi and all of them got in the car. Jeffie still had tears in his eyes, and Sandi saw them. She asked, "Are you hurt?"

Jeffie nodded.

"Where's the hurt?" Sandi wanted to know.

"In here." Jeffie pointed at his heart.

Sandi looked carefully at his shirt. "Sandi make it better?" she asked hopefully.

"Yes," said Jeffie. "Sandi *did* make it better. But sometimes it still hurts."

They drove quietly to the little country

graveyard where Morrie rested. Mama slowly drove down the gravel road. Queen Anne's lace and other wildflowers seemed to wave as they went by. The car stopped in a parking place.

"Can I take Sandi up to see the grave, by myself?" Jeffie asked.

Mom nodded. "I'll just wait here in the car."

So Jeffie and Sandi walked up the little hill, past many gravestones, until they came to a small white one with a lamb on top. Morrie's name was on the stone. Jeffie knelt in the grass and drew Sandi down beside him.

"It's hard for you to understand, Sandi," he said. "But before you came, I had a little brother. His name was Morrie. He was a nice little boy and we were good friends. One day he got sick. First he went to a hospital. Then he died. He will never come back. He is gone. We buried him here." Jeffie patted the ground. "Right here."

He looked at his sister. Her dark eyes were serious. She was listening carefully.

"Since you came, Sandi, I haven't felt so sad anymore," he said. "But sometimes I still miss Morrie."

"Morrie's all gone?" Sandi asked anxiously.

"All gone," said Jeffie.

"My mommy's all gone, too," Sandi said sadly. "My daddy's all gone, too."

With amazement Jeffie realized that Sandi still remembered her birth parents. She still missed them! She had been only 2 when they died. He looked at her face, and saw the same sadness there that he often felt for Morrie. Tears filled Sandi's eyes, and then Jeffie's, as they remembered the ones they had lost.

Then Jeffie said, "Sandi, did you know that when Jesus comes, He's going to wake them up again?"

"Jesus will?"

"Yes, He is going to wake up all the good people. Then we will see them again. I want to see your mommy and daddy and tell them what a nice girl you are. And you can see Morrie, and tell him what a nice boy I am," he added, grinning.

Sandi giggled. "I will tell Morrie you are a *nice boy!*" she said firmly. "A *very nice boy!*"

"Let's put a flower here for Morrie," Jeffie said. "I always do. And let's put one here for your mommy and daddy, too. They can't see them," he explained, "but God does. He knows that we don't forget them."

"I don't forget," said Sandi, picking as many

daisies and dandelions as she could get her hands on.

They put the flowers on Morrie's grave, and Jeffie said, "I feel better now. Don't the flowers look pretty?"

"Mmm-hmm," said Sandi.

Jeffie took Sandi's hand and together they walked back to the car. Perhaps they would come again, some time soon. Or maybe it would be a long time. Mom always said, "Time is different to God. In His sight, Morrie is just having a little nap."

It was quiet and early afternoon when they got back home. Sandi was sleepy, so she lay down for a nap. Jeffie ate a sandwich, then wandered out to sit in the swing. For quite a while he swung and watched Charley switch away flies with his long tail. Jeffie looked over where the green leaves had been—the ones that had no flowers. Mom had said, "Just wait."

Jeffie thought about the plant. *It was just like Morrie,* he thought. *He just got started as a kid, and then he died.* He got up and walked over to the spot. He thought he'd see the dry brown earth of summer.

Instead he saw a thick, shiny stalk with a

large pink bud. And there was another, and another! Every place there'd been leaves, Jeffie saw flower stalks. And some had bloomed. The big pink trumpets filled the air with sweet perfume.

"They're called resurrection lilies," said Mom, who'd come up quietly behind him.

"Wow!" Jeff said softly. "These are beautiful. I thought they were dead."

"Yes, when the leaves die down, it looks as if they're dead. But in late summer they rise again. I planted them to remind us that even when it seems as if death has won, Jesus has the last word."

They heard a small sound and turned to see Sandi in the doorway, rubbing her sleepy eyes. As Jeffie went to her, he knew that life had come back to him, too.

"Come, Sandi," he said gently, taking her hand. "Come with me and see the flowers."